COPTIC ORTHODOX PATRIARCHATE

See of St. Mark

WORDS
OF
SPIRITUAL BENEFIT

Volume IV
(151 - 200)

BY
H. H. POPE SHENOUDA III

Published By

C.O.P.T.

First Edition 1989

H.H. Pope Shenouda III, 117th Pope of Alexandria and the See of St. Mark

This book was printed
on the occasion of
the historic

Papal Visit

Australia 1989

by

His Holiness Pope Shenouda Ill
Patriarch of the See of St Mark

CONTENTS

In the name of the Father,
the Son and the Holy Spirit
One God, Amen.

PREFACE

When we started this series we did not expect that we will reach 200 words and a fourth volume. But we thank God who completed these words for us.

They are words on many different topics which are not meant to be divided into parts and chapters. But they are spiritual contemplations, which you can read without keeping a specific order.

You can obtain what is missing from the previous three volumes in order to complete the series.

SHENOUDA III

1st July 1986 (24 Baounah)
Feast of St Moses the Black

151. STATE OF BALANCE (EQUILIBRIUM)

Many are those who, in their spiritual lives, tend to the extreme right or to the extreme left, swinging between two opposites.

And few are those who keep the balance and stay firm in it.

For example, the spiritual persons who fast in devoutness during the passion week, loosen their will completely and eat without control in the fifty days which follow Easter; what they gained during fasting they entirely lose because there is no balance in their lives.

The same applies to silence and talk: they may go on a complete silence exercise, talking to no one. And when such exercise comes to an end, they return to talking with all its wrongs and without vigilance.

The right procedure for a spiritual person is to keep his balance in silence and talk; to know when to stop and when to talk and if he speaks, what are his limits.

Also, a person needs balance in the handling of people. Many cannot keep the balance between humility and courage in their life.

They might exaggerate in their humility until it turns into weakness and leniency, or exaggerate in their courage until it turns into rashness and imprudence. A spiritual person must be humble in his courage and courageous in his humility and combine wisdom with both.

Also, in the upbringing of children, there has to be a balance between pampering and harshness.

Some see love as pampering and continual giving without wisdom or control; and compassion which encourages the continuity of wrong doings without mindfulness. But, balance is in the loving firmness and in the firm love.

Balance holds in itself a lot of wisdom, understanding what it should be without right or left exaggeration.

It is said by some wise men that virtue is the middle position between two opposites, between intemperance and temperance.

Balance helps one to be firm because extravagance based on rashness cannot be stable and it is easy to change to the contrary.

Search for such balance in all details of your spiritual life.

152.   THE TRUTH

He who loves and always defends the truth, before he takes God's rights from people, he must first take God's right from himself.

He who loves the truth, never favours himself or any of his beloved ones on the account of truth, because he loves the truth from all his heart more than he loves anyone.

The lover of truth has only scales to weigh for all, he does not strain out a gnat for one and he does not swallow a camel for the other.

He does not condemn anyone for something which he justifies for another because of his feelings towards this or that.

He has no objection to take the blame and refuse to justify himself as he considers that self-justification does not agree with the truth and it puts in front of him the Lord's saying: *"He who justifies the wicked and he who condemns the just, both of them alike are an abomination to the Lord." (Prov. 17:15).*

He who loves the truth never oppresses anyone and does not accept someone to suffer injustice, even those who are against him.

He loves the truth far from any denomination and discrimination, with no difference between a relative or a stranger. To him, the truth does not differ because of religion, sex or relationship.

Truth is one of God's names and he who loves the truth, loves God and who keeps away from the truth, keeps away from God.

He who is led by the truth will be pleased with its leadership and nourishment and lives by it.

153. YOUR COMFORT AND THE COMFORT OF OTHERS

A noble person does not build his comfort on the weariness of others. But the noble one is he who sacrifices his comfort in order to comfort others.

A mother might feel comfort in having her son by her side while the son, at the same time, might find comfort in being far from home. He might travel, migrate, become a monk or live on his own with a wife. Here, the noble mother would let him go without insisting on her comfort by his side.

Your comfort could be in amusing yourself, raising your voice, raising the volume of your radio or television. But the noble one sacrifices all that if others need quietness to study, to sleep, or to recover from sickness. It is not proper to deprive others of their comfort for your own enjoyment.

You might find comfort in releasing what is inside you through criticism; then you hurt the feelings of others. But the noble one would not do this.

Many noble persons with big hearts never wish to compete with others in any field. Because of their love for others and forsaking what they want, they leave the field for them.

As said by one of the saints, *"Forsake what is in people's hands, people will love you."*

A noble person remains silent to give others a chance to talk. But if others wanted to listen to him, then he speaks.

That does not mean a noble person acts according to peoples wishes, whatever they are! Of course not. If people find comfort in what is wrong, he would not share it with them, because to please God is more important than pleasing people. And because he wants the real comfort for people, it would not be by encouraging them to do what is wrong.

Therefore, try to gain people according to your capacity, provided that you gain your conscience too. Avoid pampering that could spoil those who are younger than you, or obedience that could corrupt those who are older than you. If you fail to comfort someone by fulfilling his wrong wishes, try to comfort him morally by conviction or by a cheerful word.

As the Bible says, *"If it is possible, as much as depends on you, live peaceably with all men."* (Rom. 12:18).

154. MANY WATERS

The Song of Songs tells, *"Many waters cannot quench love, nor can the floods drown it." (Song 8:7).*

The same applies to the love between God and man and also to the love between man and his brother.

If love is strong and firm, the outer factors will never shake it, no matter what they are; it is like a house built on the rocks. Look at Christ's love for His disciples. It never changed or weakened. Peter denied Him thrice and the Lord still told Him, *"Feed my lambs", "Tend my sheep".* Thomas doubted Him but He did not become angry with him. He appeared to him and strengthened his faith, the same with Mary Magdalene. The disciples scattered when the Lord was arrested, but His love for them remained as it was.

It is the same with God's love that He showed towards the world that sinned. And towards those who rejected Him, he continued offering His hand, knocking on their doors and sending His prophets to them.

Finally, *"God demonstrated His own love towards us, in that while we were still sinners, Christ died for us." (Rom. 5: 8).*

As for you, is your love for God firm? Or does your love shake when faced by many waters? Such as a trial, tribulation, sickness, death or when confronted by some concerns or doubts? Or may be some sins, desires or stumbling blocks?

Look at St. Paul the Apostle who says, *"who shall separate us from the love of Christ?... Neither death or life, nor things present nor things to come, nor tribulation or distress or persecution." (Rom. 8:35-39).*

Is your love for friends and favoured ones: also firm?

Or could any specific event make your heart change towards a love that you had for many years? That is what sometimes happens in a family which makes it collapse and separate after many years. It fails to hold fast against the water, even if it is not many waters.

Does your love change because of a word that did not please your ears? Or a behaviour that annoyed you? Or the effect of others on you? Or for external circumstances, or financial reasons? Then the words of the Bible echo in your ears, *"nevertheless, I have this against you, that you have left your first love." (Rev. 2:4).*

155. LOVE ENDURES ALL THINGS

Everybody could respond to the type of love that gives and sacrifices that comforts and cheers all who meet with it.

But could everybody endure others if they do wrong against them, without losing love because of an offence, or what was considered to be an offence?

The apostle Paul says, *"love bears all things .... love never fails."* Many waters cannot quench love. (1 Cor. 13:7-8). All the sins of people did not change the love of God, who, while we were still sinners died for us. Peter's denial of Jesus could not change the Lord's love for Peter and it remained as it was.

All the wrong doings of Absalom, his betrayal and war against his father, never changed David's love for him. David not only tolerated him but said, *"Beware lest anyone touch the young man Absalom .... the king was deeply moved and went up to the chamber and wept." (2 Sam. 18:12).*

As David's love endured Absalom, it also endured the king and all his troubles. How touching was David's lamentation of Saul who repeatedly attempted to kill him .

17

Look at the mother's love for her son it never fails, no matter how the son would err. She endures everything he does and her love remains as it is. It is the love that does not seek its own and bears all things.

As for the one who is self-centred, he never knows love as it should be. And if he does love, his love would not be capable of enduring as it should be.

Bear the faults of others as God bears your faults.

Bear, but not in distress and bitterness of heart but in love, feeling that everyone has his own weaknesses. Maybe he also has his own excuses that you do not know.

Examine your love by endurance, to know the extent of its soundness.

156. THE TEMPLE OF THE SPIRIT

The apostle said, *"Do you not know that you are the temple of God and that the Spirit of God dwells in you?" (1 Cor. 3:16).* He also said, *"Or do you not know that your body is the temple of the Holy Spirit who is in you, whom you have from God and you are not your own?.... therefore glorify God in your body and in your Spirit, which are God's." (1 Cor. 6:19-20).*

How does one keep himself as a temple of God?

How can it be a holy house of God? When we would say with the Psalmist, *"Holiness adorns your house, O Lord." (Ps. 93:5).*

On the negative side, one avoids whatever defiles the body; not only well known sexual sins but even other sins, as the Lord said, *".... what comes out of the mouth, this defiles a man ....but those things which proceed out of the mouth come from the heart and they defile a man. For out of the heart proceed evil thoughts .... these are the things that defile a man." (Matt. 15:11-20).*

If one lived in communion with the Holy Spirit, he will avoid all these negatives because there is no association between light and darkness.

And if one lived in sin he would not be acting according to the Spirit and he would not have given the Holy Spirit a chance to work in him. But he would have *".... grieved the Holy Spirit." (Eph. 4:30) and, ".... quenched the Spirit." (1 Thess. 5:19).*

Would man in this case be a temple of God?

Or would the apostle's saying apply to him, *"If anyone defiles the temple of God, God will destroy him. For the temple of God is Holy, which temple you are." (1 Cor. 3:17).*

And if one is a temple of God what comes out of this temple would be, *"psalms, hymns and spiritual songs." (Eph. 5:19).*

As well as that, if man is a temple of God, all his life will be transformed into a holy sacrifice, a pleasing aroma for God. And as the apostle said, *"present your bodies a living sacrifice." (Rom. 12:1).*

And if one is a temple for the Spirit the fruits of the Spirit will show in him. His whole life becomes holy. Spirituality will show in everything he does and God will be glorified through him. He will also be given the power about which God said, *"But you will receive power when the Holy Spirit has come upon you." (Acts 1:8).*

157. GOD AND MAN

The most ancient and the most permanent relationship is that between God and man.

It is an eternal relationship since we were an idea in His mind and a pleasure in His heart. It is an everlasting relationship because it never ends.

As for the relationship between human beings they are bound to a certain period of time, a specific place on earth and a special purpose.

The relationship between humans could remain forever if they share in doing what is good and in pleasing God. By doing this they will be allowed to meet together in the bosom of God, in eternity.

Therefore, a firm, permanent relationship is that with God.

The relationship among humans could also be firm and permanent if God is one party in it. Also, if this relationship is connected to one of God's commandments, or one of the sublime values that God set as a rule for dealings between people; otherwise anything else is perishable.

If that is how the relationship with God is, then it should be placed on top of our concerns, giving it priority over everything and everyone else, also choosing it before the self and all its demands.

If God's love clashes with any other type of love, place God before all, as He said with His pure mouth, *"He who loves father or mother more than me is not worthy of me."* (Matt. 10:37).

Therefore, we should not love a person or try to please somebody on account of our love for God. As the apostle said, *"For if I still pleased men, I would not be a servant of Christ."* (1 Gal. 1:10).

For God's sake one should even be prepared to deny himself and carry his cross.

Those who love God with all the heart and all the thought, according to the commandment, devote themselves completely like the ascetic fathers. Their motto was, "Leaving everyone for the ONE."

Let God be to us, not only first but all. He is the one with whom we will live in eternity. Our love for Him decides our destiny and outlines the nature of our lives.

158. THE STRONG HEART

The strong heart is the firm heart which exterior factors cannot overcome. It does not shake because of anything on the outside.

The strong heart does not change from a word, no matter how cruel it was, it would not be disturbed by any treatment, no matter how unusual. This heart would not be enticed by any temptations and is never shaken by any agitations. It is persistent, controlled only by the principles that he believes in and the ideals that he holds fast to.

The strong heart never changes because of pride, money, position, materialistic or spiritual dignity. At the same time, the opposite of all these would not make it fall into little spirit.

The strong heart is never overcome by worry or despair, nor by disturbance or fear. But it listens to the apostle's saying, *"Be steadfast, immovable." (1 Cor. 15:58).*

The strength of the heart has reasons, some of it natural and others a blessing.

There is a person whose heart is strong by nature. He is like a lion with courage and bravery without fear. But he might be spiritual and he might not. He might show strength on certain occasions only, then he might weaken when faced by external factors. He might also weaken because of a desire he could not resist.

Another person would have the reason of his strength centralised in his spirituality.

The one who abandons everything is always strong. He does not covet anything or long for anything. He does not have a point of weakness that the enemy could take advantage of. As St. Augustine said, *"I sat on top of the world when I felt that I desired nothing and feared nothing."*

One's strength could be in love for eternity since death itself never frightened him. Or his love for the truth could be the reason for his strong heart. Truth is always strong, no matter what clashes with it.

And the reason for strength of the heart could be Faith.

Faith in God's power that is with you, guards and protects you and gives you help from the Holy Spirit. As the Lord said, *"But you will receive power when the Holy Spirit has come upon you." (Acts 1:8).* And as St. Paul said, *"I can do all things through Christ who strengthens me." (Phil. 4:13).*

159. ETERNITY

Man's limited life on earth, if compared with eternity which is unlimited, will revert to a zero, as if it is nothing.

In spite of that, people worry about their life on earth as if it is everything for them. They devote their emotions, time and effort for it. They even give it the first place in their hearts, whether it is their life on earth or it is the life of their dear ones, relatives, friends or acquaintances.

In all that, they forget their eternity and the eternity of others.
To pay attention to eternity, you have to be convinced of it and think of it. You have to labour for it with all your strength and make it your heart's concern.

The holy church puts this aim in front of us in the Agbia prayers, especially in the compline and midnight prayers. It is also in the sunset prayer and in many psalms. All of that is meant to keep this subject of eternity always in our mind.

For that reason, the Lord Jesus Christ said, "For what will it profit a man if he gains the whole world and loses his own soul?" (Mark 8:36).

St. Paul the apostle also said, *"While we do not look at the things that are seen, but at the things which are not seen. For the things which are seen are temporary, but the things which are not seen are eternal." (2 Cor. 4:18).*

For this eternity that is not seen now, our fathers the saints lived a life of deprivation and death to the world. They concentrated with all their hearts and emotions on the love of God alone. They longed for Him and for an eternal life with Him. And so they started their way towards eternity and departure from this world. They were rewarded by tasting God's kingdom.

The one who works for his eternity does not love the world or the things that are in it; confident that the world is passing away and the lust of it too.

The one who works for his eternity always acts carefully in everything, lest he loses his crown through a mistake or neglect.

And the one who prepares himself for eternity thinks much of the world to come, of God, His angels and His saints. He thinks of God's dwelling with people, in the Heavenly Jerusalem, in the release of the Spirit from the heaviness of the body. He sees that this is much better and longs for it.

160. SILENCE

Silence, in its primary stage, is avoiding the mistakes of the tongue. As the Book says, *"In the multitude of words, sin is not lacking." (Prov. 10:19).* "Many a time I have spoken and regretted it" says St. Arsanius, "but as for my silence, never did I regret it."

Silence, from another point, is leaving aside human effort, giving God a chance to work. As the Bible says, *"Stand still and see the salvation of the Lord." (Exo. 14:13).* And, *"The Lord will fight for you and you shall hold your peace." (Exo. 14:14).*

Silence is sometimes a kind of composure and not to revenge for oneself or repay evil for evil. The Lord Jesus Christ was afflicted, yet He opened not His mouth, (Is. 53:7). And during His trial, He was silent both when He faced the Sanhedrin, Annanias, Caiaphas and Pilate.

There was power in His silence to the extent that Pilate, the governor said, *"I have no fault in this just Man." (Luke 23:14).*
Silence also gives a chance for prayer and contemplation.
The one who talks much never gets a chance to pray and does not have the capacity for interior spiritual work.

One of the saints was right in saying, "The one who talks much proves that he is empty inside," which means void of interior spiritual work.

When St. Arsanius was asked about his silence and isolation he replied, "I cannot be with God and with people at the same time."

What a beautiful saying is that of St. John saba "Silence your tongue to let your heart speak and silence your heart to let God speak."

Silence covers many types, such as: silence of the tongue and silence of the senses, because if the senses were occupied without the control of man, they would bring thoughts that would hinder him from prayer and contemplation. The one who wants to be silent in a spiritual manner, has to guard his sight, hearing and the rest of his senses.

Silence teaches one to be serious and quiet. It keeps him far from clamour, uproar and noise. It also avoids him mixing with many ideas that could distract the thought making it hard to be recollected at time of prayer.

Silence also goes with being alone, without too much mixing with others.

161. MULTITUDE OF WORDS

There are people who concentrate heavily on their talk, in a way that makes it need more clarification and analysis to be understood by the listener.

To the opposite of that, there are those who carry on talking unnecessarily and what is said could be summed up in a quarter or a tenth or even less. That is what we want to talk about. The reason for a multitude of words could be repetition, by repeating same words, same phrase, same expression or the whole story.

The reason could also be to explain and clarify what has been said, as if the listener lacks good understanding and comprehension! Or the lengthening could be from inside, by too many boring details.

Maybe the whole topic is not important, or at least is not worth the time spent on it.

And the reason for a multitude of words could be the enthusiasm of the speaker for a specific matter and he or she wants to pass this enthusiasm to the listener, thinking that by a multitude of words on that topic, the listener will be convinced and show interest!

The listener maybe convinced but the speaker continues talking, either to stress confirmation and conviction or because he believes that what he will say is important and he must say it. It could also be energy inside him and he will never rest without emptying it.

Maybe it is just the nature of the speaker, to repeat and increase in his talk, about anything!

Extending the talk could lead to boredom and weariness, so the listener loses interest or tries to get rid of that talk somehow. He could also try to avoid the speaker whenever he meets him, if it is in his nature to use a multitude of words.

Using a multitude of words means lack of concern for the time and commitments of the listener. It also means ignoring his psychology, nerves and his way of understanding.

Therefore, train your self to measure your words. Notice your listener and do not allow him to get bored of your talk. And if he understands your aim, there is no need to repeat or extend.

Do not give a topic more time than it deserves. Avoid talking about trivial matters.

162. WHY DID THEY LOVE MARTYRDOM?

Our fathers the martyrs received martyrdom, not only in tolerance and satisfaction, but mostly with joy. Thousands of the faithful travelled from Damanhore to Alexandria to be martyred. Along the way they sang chants joyfully.

It was also said about the twelve Apostles that when they were flogged and thrown in prison, *"They departed, rejoicing that they were counted worthy to suffer shame for His name." (Acts 5:41).*

St. Abu Pham the soldier, when he was called for martyrdom, he dressed up in his best attire saying, "This is my wedding day."

Why were our fathers joyful about martyrdom?

> They considered martyrdom the shortest way leading to the joys of heaven. It is a matter of moments or hours, then one will be in the bosom of Abraham, Isaac and Jacob in the assembly of the saints.

Therefore, in the story of the martyrdom of St. Ighnatios of Antioch, when the people of Rome wanted to kidnap him to save him from death, he sent them a message to stop them from doing that, saying "My beloved, I am afraid that your love will do me harm and after I reach my destination, I'll turn back my life-journey all over again."

They also looked at martyrdom as means of sharing in Christ's passion, in His death and subsequently in His glory.

They used to look at the Bible's saying, *"If indeed we suffer with Him, we may also be glorified together." (Rom. 8:17).*

Some of them personally saw the crowns that they were striving to receive.

Or saw the crowns of those who were martyred before them.

And without seeing anything, they were confident through faith, of what God has prepared for those who love His Holy name, those who accept suffering for His sake.

They also used to look at martyrdom as the best way to express their love for God and the truth of their faith. And as it says in the Bible, *"Greater love has no one than this, to lay down His life for His friends." (John 15:13).* How much more deserving then for faith.

They loved martyrdom because they were certain of being strangers in this world. They also loved eternity in a way that took hold over their hearts and they never looked at death except as a release from the prison of the body.

163. SELF-EXPRESSION

One may fail in his relationships with others, not because of bad intentions but because of bad expression.

Good intentions alone are not enough, if one does not express them in good words that will leave good effect on oneself.

Therefore, the one who knows how to choose expressions in his talk is most of the time successful in his relationship with people.

As the Bible says, *"For by your words you will be justified and by your words you will be condemned." (Matt. 12:37).* These words could also mean that "By your words people will love you or hate you."

Many beneficial and sincere advices were rejected by people in spite of their wisdom and benefit. That is because the advice was offered in harsh words that turned them off. They could not find in it the love that would make them listen to it.

What matters most is not the specific and correct meaning of what you are saying but putting it in an appealing manner that makes it acceptable by the listener.

Some might ask, "Is it permissible to criticise the behaviour of others, justify it or comment on it if we are in a responsible position and it is meant for the general good?" Or we should avoid that for fear of provoking those we criticise? This, in fact, also depends on the expression used.

One could say exactly what he wants without anybody getting angry with him. They will probably thank him, as it happened with Abigail and David. She managed to give him rebuke, warning and advice in an atmosphere of pure praise, love, respect and gratitude, till he said to her, *"Blessed are you and blessed is your advice." (1 Sam. 25:33)*.

Another person would only say a few words, but the world would turn upside down as a result of that, causing problems and crises. That is just because these words were not well chosen and the expression was bad.

Therefore, I advise you to choose your expressions and be specific in using words, because "Your language reveals you."

That is not only to develop good relations with others but also for the sake of having a pure heart, as God's son.

164. THE LIFE OF FAITH

Many people believe in God just on the surface, or through the mind only. As for the practical side, this does not exist.

One is counted among the faithful but does not have the heart of the faithful.

What is faith then? And how do we live in it? *"Now faith is the substance of things hoped for, the evidence of things not seen." (Heb. 11:1).*

It is then a level higher than the senses.

The senses are too weak to understand. Faith does not contradict the senses but has a higher level than them.

We believe in God without seeing Him. We believe in the angels surrounding us without seeing them. We believe in God's work and promises without linking that to our senses, our mind or our thought.

Faith also has a higher level than that of the mind. Therefore, we also believe in miracles and wonders.

The mind might not understand the miracles but would accept them without linking acceptance to understanding something on a higher level. It was given the name miracle because it indicates the inability of the mind to understand or analyse what happens.

By having faith in God and His protection, we depend on Him confidently.

This dependence could reach complete submission where our life is fully handed over to God in confidence that what He does is for our good. We don't have to see what He does. It is enough to believe without seeing, as God says, *"Blessed are those who have not seen and yet have believed." (John 20:29).*

The faithful is the one whose heart is always comforted and has no fear.

When Peter feared, the Lord said to him, *"O you of little faith, why did you doubt?" (Matt. 14:31).* The doubt and fear are the outcome of a weak faith. The faithful is strong and never weakens before any situation.

How beautiful is the Bible's saying, *"All things are possible to him who believes." (Mark 9:23).*

St. Paul the faithful says, *"I can do all things in Christ who strengthens me." (Phil. 4:13).*

What else could be said about faith?

The life of faith could include the whole spiritual life.

165. THE WORD IS A RESPONSIBILITY

Any intelligent person searches, with all his might, for a word of benefit. As the word is for benefit, it is of responsibility.

The Bible says, *"For everyone to whom much is given, from him much will be required." (Luke 12:48).*

Ignorance is the sin of the one who does not know. As for the one who knows, his sin is premeditated and is of an evil intention and his responsibility is greater. Therefore, the sin of preachers, teachers and priests is greater than the sin of the congregation. The priest says in the offertory, "For my sins and the ignorance of Your people". To him, they are sins but to those who didn't know, it is ignorance.

What then? Is it better for one not to know so his sins will be less? St. Augustine here says, "There is a big difference between the one who does not know and the one who refuses to know. The one who rejects knowledge will be judged for his rejection."

The one who refuses to know God and His ways also proves that he does not love God and does not deserve Him.

What about the responsibility?

It is true that knowledge is a responsibility. But with knowledge comes a divine support that helps those who know to carry out and apply.

With the word comes strength, therefore it is said that the word is alive and effective. *"For the Word of God is living and powerful and sharper than any two edged sword." (Heb. 4:12).*

When one accepts the word of knowledge, he also accepts God who gave it and also the Holy Spirit that gives strength and encouragement to carry it out. That is how God's word was at the time of the Apostles. With one word from Peter, three thousand believed. And the word said by St. Stephen could not be resisted by the three councils. Therefore, ask for the strength of the word to work in you.

God's word has its effect on the conscience. It illuminates and also kindles it. It stimulates it to do good and protests against any mistake.

God's word will always follow you pressing you. No matter how much you shall resist, it will surely come back to you even after a long time and stand before you.

The Lord says, *"So shall my word be that goes forth from my mouth. It shall not return to me void." (Is. 55:11).*

166. THE TRANSFIGURATION

The transfiguration of Jesus Christ with both Moses and Elijah was a token for the transfiguration of humanity as a whole.

This transfiguration is a release for our nature from materialism and its weight.

It is also a promise from the Lord to save our nature from the slavery of corruption, the slavery of the substance, to become spiritual and luminous. Then we become worthy of living in the kingdom that is prepared for us.

In eternity, we will be free from the slavery of flesh and blood and what they demand. We will be like God's angels in heaven.

But this transfiguration will be granted only to the one who never submitted to substance during his life on earth. He will become luminous in eternity.

There are also those who will become luminous because during their life on earth they acted as the children of light and never dealt with acts of darkness that are fruitless. On the contrary, they followed the saying, *"Walk as children of light. And have no fellowship with the unfruitful works of darkness, but rather expose them." (Eph. 5:11).*

That is because those who had fellowship with the works of darkness will be thrown out in the outside darkness of eternity, far from the city of light and the fellowship of the luminous in heavenly Jerusalem.

Transfiguration in eternity is not going to be only for the body but also for the spirit. And so we will be released from the defile of the body and spirit. Transfiguration of the spirit means to be crowned with righteousness, so fault and sin would not have any authority over man any more.

This transfiguration is our return to God's image.

Adam and Eve were created to God's image in purity, righteousness and simplicity. But the transfiguration in eternity will take a more sublime way than the nature of Adam and Eve. Humans will be released from the materialism of the body and become spiritual and closer to God's image as on the Mount of Tabor.

Would we prepare ourselves now to become worthy of this transfiguration, by acting according to the spirit. So we become worthy of having spiritual bodies in eternity, like God's angels in heaven.

The Feast of the Transfiguration calls us to the spiritual life.

167. RESPECTING OTHERS

Respect others and others will respect you.

Respect others for their humanity, whatever the age, position or social status, just for being humans like you.

Respecting the old is a matter that all people practically practise. They feel it is a duty and obligation neglected only by the rebellious.

As for respecting the young, it is a matter urged by nobility.

When do you feel spiritually obliged to respect your son, your subordinates at work, your servant and those who are lower than your cultural or economic level?

Your respect to people makes you gain their love and you don't lose your reverence.

Respecting people has two sides: one is negative and the other is positive.

As for the negative side, it is by avoiding insulting words and sarcasm. It is also refraining from using cruel words or behaviour that could hurt feelings.

The positive side is making the other person feel the love and respect that is in your heart towards them. It is also by making him feel how much he means to you and that you hold him higher than what he thinks, due to humility.

The Lord Jesus Christ said about the negative side in respecting others, *"And whoever says to his brother 'Raca!' shall be in danger of the council. But whoever says, 'You fool!' shall be in danger of hell fire."* (Matt. 5:22).

As for the positive side, the Lord Jesus Christ said to His disciples, *"No longer do I call you servants, but I have called you friends."* (John 15:15). *"You are the light of the world."* (Matt. 5:14). *"You are the salt of the earth."* (Matt. 5:13). *"Whoever honours you, honours Me."* (Luke 10:16).

It is a great shame to say, that some consider using expressions of respect between intimate friends or relatives as an artificiality that should be overcome!

In fact, expressions of respect don't ever stop feelings of love and intimacy. On the contrary, they increase love between people, make the relationship stronger and stop fraction.

It is advisable that mutual respect should be the most outstanding aspect among those who are married. It does not only link hearts, but also sets a good example for the children, teaching them how to be polite in words and in action.

168. HOW MANY ARE OUR TEACHERS?

The one who has the spirit of discipleship and likes learning and gaining a word of benefit would in no way be able to count the number of his teachers, or in other words the sources of his knowledge.

We do not mean by that, those within the family circle as parents and relatives. Or teachers at schools and universities which are many. We don't even mean those in the Church circle such as a confession father, spiritual father, clergy, church servants and all preachers or teachers of the theological college, if one had the chance to deal with them.

For each person there is a countless number of people that we learn from, about all aspects of life. It could be intentional or unintentional, whether we realise it or not.

Would anyone deny that many have affected him by their life-style, ideals, principles and behaviour, without intentionally trying to teach him. They left a permanent mark on himself and provided him with models of life that became printed on his mind?

Would you be able to count those whose lives were a beneficial lesson to you? It could be either their style of speech, their way of treating others or how they solve problems.

Would anyone deny learning from others' mistakes as well as others' ideals? Their mistakes and their outcome became loud bells, cautioning, warning and frightening him, giving him an unforgettable lesson!

As one learns from others' mistakes, no doubt he also learns from his own mistakes and from what he receives in his life of punishments, words of rebuke or words of reproach. One even learns from words of sarcasm, criticism or insult. That is, if he wants to learn.

Social relationships, with all their results are also lessons.
How many times did you learn a lesson from your dealings in life? How many advices or comments have you received from a friend or a passer by? How many lessons have you learned from those who deceived, exploited or fought you? How many lessons have you learned from those who helped you without making you aware of their help, or those who put up with you without complaining?

How many benefits have you gained, by passing by a discussion between two?

Then how many would be our teachers from the friends and enemies, alive or dead, righteous or evil, right or wrong?

There are other lessons one learns from his readings and they are many. That could be either from books, newspaper, magazines or other types of media. There are lessons from stories, plays and even jokes and comedies. Many of these have a lesson deep within.

Events are also teachers as we learn lessons from them.

How many are the lessons that people learned from death, wars, catastrophes, fraction and their outcome or from all events that God allows?

The news that we hear or read everyday has a lesson if dealing with life.

We even learn lessons from animals, birds and insects.

We learn from the ant how to be active, from the bee how to be organised, from the dog loyalty, bravery from the lion, intelligence from the serpent, patience from the fox and fasting from the camel.

Sources of knowledge are everywhere. But who is the one who wants to learn?

The world and life are large schools full of lessons.

169. SPARE TIME

The one who knows the value of time would use it for his benefit. This person would never have spare time, because his time will never be enough for the responsibilities that he has.

The one with spare time must have empty space in his life that has not been filled yet. Having emptiness in life, in aim or in ambition is really a sad matter!

Therefore, those with great endeavours never have spare time.

Those with ambitions in life, either spiritual or academic or even materialistic would have no spare time.

Spare time is the result of man's failure to know how to use his time. Once he does, this problem would not be there any more.

The problem of spare time could face the old or those who reached the retiring age and thought that their message in life has ended. Their life became without job and without aim!

Those people need to search for a job so their world does not become boring and a burden on them.

The spiritual concept of using the spare time is not to look for a way to pass time! It is looking for a way to benefit from time.

Time is a part of life and it is unlawful to kill it or waste it uselessly. That would mean that life is cheap in your eyes, as if your time has no value!!

Spare time is a problem that faces students during the summer vacation, as they finish their studies and find nothing to keep them busy as studying did before.

It is the duty of educators to organise activities to keep students busy during the summer holidays. It is also the duty of parents, the church and Sunday school.

That is why summer activities took an important scope in the mind of those in charge of the youth and the children. They put programmes for them to benefit from. By doing that, the young would not feel that the church has neglected them and left them to their own devices to pass time in any way, where they could cause themselves great harm.

The mind always works. It does not slow down or stop. If it does not think of good then it could think of evil or at least in trifles that would not build it. And so instead of facing emptiness of time, it would be facing emptiness in life and in thoughts!

The problem of spare time could face many ladies or house-wives who do not have children or their children are grown-up. Here, we repeat the question: How do we spend our spare time?

170. HOW DO WE SPEND OUR SPARE TIME?

1. There is no objection at all in having some enjoyment or relaxation. One can't continually be concentrating, serious or tense. God Himself gave days for rest and specified it to be "for man".

2. One of the useful things for spare time is reading for those who are good at it and enjoy it. The important point is choosing what is good for building one's personality, intellectually, spiritually and socially. Reading is a weapon with two edges, it could benefit and it could harm.

3. There is another method for enjoyment. It could be added to reading or replace it for those who can't read much.

   Enjoyment could be obtained from spiritual gatherings or the cassette tapes that you listen to in your car while on the road, at home while you are relaxing, when the family is all gathered or when you meet some friends.

4. In your spare time, you may view some religious films or video tapes that are shown at some churches and religious societies. Some even buy such tapes to keep at home. Some methods of passing spare time: Service.

By serving you benefit and others benefit with you. What you have missed during the year could be done during the summer vacation such as visiting, meeting those you serve, preparing lessons and visual aid for the future plus many other activities.

Group visits could be organised to look after the poor, orphanages, disabled, poor local districts plus sharing experiences among servants through visits, camps and conferences for the service.

Another method of spending spare time: Memorising, either verses from the Bible, hymns, psalms and prayers, parts from the Psalmody or the regular church chants and those used for certain occasions.

One of the beneficial ways for spare time is: periods of retreat. One may spend these periods either at monasteries or other places. But there has to be a spiritual programme to be followed so one would spiritually gain from it.

Others may use their spare time in social obligations such as delayed visits or courteous duties.

171. PEACE OF THE HEART

The spiritual person is supposed to have a heart full of peace and quietness. He is not to get disturbed on the inside or the outside, but to live in peace with himself, with people and with God.

Peace is one of the main fruits of the Holy Spirit. The Apostle says, *"But the fruit of the Spirit is love, joy, peace."* (Gal. 5:22).

What makes us lose our peace? How to win?

Sometimes we lose our peace and become annoyed when things happen different from what we want. We want to impose our will on people, events and the will of God Himself. If things happen in a different way, we lose our peace. We have to know that not all what we want could be fulfilled. May be it is for our own good that it is not.

We may lose our peace because we follow the faults of people! Even if these faults were not directed to us! We want people to act according to what we want, otherwise we get annoyed! It is better for us and for them, in order to keep our peace and theirs, to avoid interfering in other people's affairs and not to make ourselves observers of their deeds.

Losing our peace could also happen when we feel injustice and that we have been victimised. With some endurance, one can tolerate injustice without losing his peace. He may consider it a crown, believing that God *"executes justice for the oppressed." (Ps. 146:7).*

On the other hand, we should examine ourselves; may be we are wrong and there has been no injustice to make us lose our peace.

We may lose our peace because of certain desires that have not been fulfilled or may be fulfilled but not according to our expectations. But happy is the one who is pleased with what he has and does not get disturbed thinking about what he lacks. Contentment is a way to peace.

We may lose our peace because of sin or because we fear the result of sin, "There is no peace," *says the Lord, "for the wicked."* (Is. 48:22).

Sometimes we lose our peace because of our weak nerves; being very sensitive.

We need to solve our problems with our faith, our minds and our hearts, but not with our nerves. Agitated nerves never solve problems but complicate them and make us lose our peace.

Sometimes we think of the sharpness, depth and pain of the problem, so we lose our peace, get tired while it would have been better to think of a solution. If we reach one, we will be comforted.

We may lose our peace because of our wish to reach a quick solution. If it took long, we get disturbed. There are matters that need patience, long suffering and a period of time, to be solved without any worry.

Sometimes fear, tired nerves and expecting evil, exaggerate the problem so we get disturbed. The matter could be much easier than what we fear. But fear is an outstanding factor in losing patience. A frightened person imagines troubles and dangers that do not exist.

We may lose our peace because of external matters, if we are easily affected. Let us be strong in faith and in endurance, like the rock that storms strike without harming it. We should not become agitated by any word or action.

One may lose his peace because of his thoughts or his lack of intelligence. It is the type that thinks much, doubts quickly and is short of device, unable to take the right action, lacks faith in God's help and solutions.

172. SINNING AGAINST GOD

One thinks that when he sins, he is sinning against others such as the person who steals, murders or acts unjustly or that he sins against himself as in neglecting his studies, his health or wasting his future either on earth or in eternity.

But the danger in sin is that one sins against God! Therefore, David says to the Lord, *"Against you, you only, have I sinned and done this evil in your sight." (Ps. 51:4).*

David did not say that he sinned against, against Uriah the Hittite or against his personal chastity.

The same with Joseph, the righteous.

When he was tempted to sin, he refused saying, *"How can I do this great wickedness and sin against God?" (Gen. 39:9).* Joseph did not say that he would sin against Potiphar and his wife. That was how deep the understanding of Joseph the righteous.

Sin is disobeying God, defying Him and breaking His Commandments.

Therefore, the Bible said, *"Whoever commits sin also commits lawlessness and sin is lawlessness." (1 John 3:4).* It was also said, *"You who make your boast in the law, do you dishonour God through breaking the law? For "The name of God is blasphemed among the Gentiles because of you." (Rom. 2:23-24).* For that reason, *"...... sin through the commandment might become exceedingly sinful." (Rom. 7:13).*

Sin is a separation from God, getting out of His fellowship, love and kingdom, because, *"What communion has light with darkness? And what accord has Christ with Belial?" (2 Cor. 6:14-15).* The one who sins becomes separated from God like the prodigal son who separated himself from his father's house and left him.

Sin is even enmity with God because it is the love of the world. The Apostle says, *".....friendship with the world is enmity with God." (James 4:4).* It is despising God's commandment. Therefore, it was said to David the prophet, *"Why have you despised the commandment of the Lord, to do evil in His sight? .....because you have despised me and have taken the wife of Uriah the Hittite to be your wife." (2 Sam.l 12:9-10).*

Even when you sin against yourself, you are sinning against God's image. When you sin against your body, you are sinning against God's temple which is within you. Therefore, the Apostle says, *"If anyone defiles the temple of God, God will destroy him. For the temple of God is holy, which temple you are." (1 Cor. 3:17).*

Therefore, the sin is unlimited because it is against God, the unlimited.

173. METHODS OF REBUKE

Some would turn to rebuke others, acting according to the words of St. Paul the Apostle, to his disciple Timothy the bishop, *"Convince, rebuke, exhort." (2 Tim. 4:2).* Put the following points before that rebuke:

1. Does the one who rebuke have the authority to do so, as the case with St. Timothy who was a bishop? Does the rebuke come under his spiritual responsibility? Is the other person younger or older than him?

2. What is the method of rebuking? Is it with cruelty and harshness? Does it hurt feelings and humiliates? Or is it in a dislikeable way? Paul the Apostle, said to the priests of Ephesus: *"Therefore, watch and remember that for three years I did not cease to warn everyone night and day with tears." (Acts 20:31).*

3. Therefore, if you rebuke anyone, let it be with humility and love. Do not rebuke with authority and haughtiness and pride. Let your rebuke take the form of quiet advice, without hurting feelings.

4. Do not reprimand those under your authority over every mistake. David the prophet says to the Lord, *"If you, Lord, shall mark iniquities, O Lord, who could stand? But there is*

forgiveness with you." (Ps. 130:3-4). To rebuke over every mistake could cause others into littleness and you'll appear before them as one who is waiting for a mistake.

5. Do not rebuke in the presence of others. That causes embarrassment. The only exception, as in the Bible, is what relates to sins known by all. The reckless who carelessly sins before all should be dealt with as the Apostle says, " *....rebuke in the presence of all, that the rest also may fear." (1 Tim. 5:20).* As for the sins that occur in private, rebuke over it in private.

6. Let your rebuke be by conviction and love: Convince the one you rebuke that you love him and fear for him and that your words are meant for his own good. Make him feel that your rebuke is not the result of enmity or despise!

7. Your rebuke could be done in an indirect way: Use the method of hinting more than being open. Or let it be in a positive way by explaining the benefits of the spiritual way which is the opposite of what happened.

8. Rebuke could be preceded by praise and followed by encouragement. The Lord followed this way with the Samaritan woman, without hurting her feelings. (John 3:17-18).

174. REVEALS HIS ORIGIN

Man continues in hiding with unknown ins and outs and his reality remains unknown till he starts dealing in the practical experience, then it reveals him.

We do not mean the experience of many years but in one incident he could be uncovered, such as what happened with Adam and Eve.

Or maybe something new enters his life and his inside starts showing.

1. For example, becoming rich. His wealth reveals him and shows qualities that were not obvious before, as the poet says: "When my friend became a man of wealth I became sure that I lost my friend". Money could show that this person has stinginess, extravagancy or desires. It also could show if he has generosity, charity or compassion. Money could also show if he has the tendency to use his wealth as means of control.

2. This person could also be revealed by holding a position or authority. It shows if he has pride, self-conceit, predominance, self-assertion, cruelty or violence, bias or injustice. All these are revealed by high position and authority.

It also shows if he is capable, gifted or uses authority for what is good, beneficial and for the love of people.

It could also show if this person has incapability, misbehaviour or mismanagement.

3. Talking also reveals one's mentality and knowledge: You don't know the reality of a taciturn person. Once he speaks, his talk reveals him. His language shows him. Therefore, the Bible says, "If the ignorant does not talk, he will be considered wise."

4. Tribulations also reveal the nature of the one facing them: One problem a person faces could reveal his reality if he is strong and endures, intelligent and acts well or gets disturbed and troubled, fears, worries, despairs quickly or collapses.

5. Another person is revealed by marriage or general dealings with others: Before that, nobody knew his reality. They knew him after he dealt with others, his wife, his mother-in-law or his family life.

6. One may talk theoretically about principles and ideals. But when given the chance to apply what he believes in, his reality will be revealed.

175.   AIMS AND MEANS

In all man's acts, it is not enough that the aim has to be holy, but also the means must be sound. Very often, man errs and fails because his means are wrong.

For example, a father wishes to raise and keep his daughter in good manners. Undoubtedly, this is a very good case, but, this father might be at fault if he resorts to revolting means to achieve his aim, ie. cruelty, detention, supervision and close watch of movements. This would make the daughter feel as if in prison and her father is the jailer.

The same applies to those who keep discipline at the churches: Surely it is a good thing, but the fault comes from the means itself; if it includes domination, harshness, rebuke, loud voice, unnecessary force or pressure, which is definitely not required to keep discipline.

Under this topic, comes mistakes in preaching: To call people to virtue and good behaviour is an undebatable sound cause and to take interest in this by preaching is a kind of a holy zeal, but the fault comes from the means, especially if it includes sarcasm, abuse, biting remark or exaggeration. If the teaching was based on unacceptable literalism and non-consideration of people's circumstances and activities or bind them with heavy burdens, hard to bear, as the Pharisees used to do. (Matt 23:4).

It is assumed that the means to a holy objective must be faultless and holy, especially in the religious sphere, or if it proceeded from the clergy. The Bible said, *"And he who wins souls is wise." (Prov. 11:30).* Also, *"If a man is overtaken in any trespass, you who are spiritual, restore such a person in a spirit of gentleness." (Gal. 6:1).*

" ... done in the meekness of wisdom." (James 3:13).

"Let all that you do be done in love." (1 Cor. 16:14).

Love, gentleness and wisdom are of the sound and lovable means.

176. WHO IS THE GREATEST?

It is not merely the aged person.

Because God lifted this rule when He chose young people and put them in leading and important positions.

He chose little David, the youngest of his brothers, favoured him over the seven elders, anointed him King over his people and the Spirit of the Lord came upon him *(1 Sam. 16:13)*.

He chose young Joseph and made him father to Pharaoh and lord of all his house *(Gen. 45:8)*. All his brothers come to bow down to the earth before him. *(Gen. 37:9-10)*.

The Lord chose Levi's tribe for priesthood and Judah's tribe for ruling and He did not choose Reuben the first born. *(Gen. 49:3,4,8)*.

He chose Jacob - who is younger than Esau - to be told in the blessing, *"Be master over your brethren and let your mother's sons bow down to you." (Gen. 27:29)*.

He chose John the Baptist, who came late after all the prophets of the Old Testament and said about him: *"Assuredly, I say to you, among those born of women there has not risen one greater than John the Baptist." (Matt. 11:11)*.

Then who is the greatest in relation to the Divine measures?

The greatest is the one whose heart is big and his love is great.

He is the one who - by the blessing working in him - can be bigger than sin, greater in his soul and ideals.

The greatest is also the brainy, who is great in his wisdom and selection.

In short, he is the greater in his personalty not the older in his age.

St. Paul was not senior among the apostles and not the first in the missionaries. He was not among the twelve disciples or the chosen seventy, nevertheless, he was able to say, *"... but I laboured more abundantly than they all." (1 Cor. 15:10)* and although he came last, yet he became an apostle to the Gentiles.

Therefore, do not be proud that you are senior because of advanced age or long service, but be great in the depth of your service and the effect of your personality on others. Be great in your sacrifice and giving; great in the harvest which the Lord gather from your land.

177. WHO HAS EARS

The Lord Jesus said, *"He who has ears to hear, let him hear."* *(Matt. 13:43)* because there are those who have ears but do not hear. For those, the Lord said, *"... because seeing they do not see and hearing they do not hear, nor do they understand." (Matt. 13:13)* and in them the prophecy of Isaiah was fulfilled: *"Make the heart of this people dull and their ears heavy." (Is. 6:10).*

Then what are the reasons that they have ears but do not hear?

Firstly, because their hearts hardened and their love diminished. He who loves God, likes to hear about Him. If he loses such love, or his heart was filled with a contrary love, he would not like to hear about God or virtue listening becomes hard on his ears.

If something is said to him, it will not go through his ears, his mind or his heart. It is not to his liking like the rich young man *(Matt. 19:22).*

"Listening but do not hear" like the people of Sodom when they were warned by Lot. *"But to his son-in-law he seemed to be joking." (Gen. 19:14).*

Or like the Epicurean and Stoic philosophers to whom Paul the Apostle spoke and they said *"What does this babbler want to say?" (Acts 17:18).*

This reminds us that pride blocks up the ear from listening.

The "Ego" stands against hearing the word of God. Likewise, the words of Christ disclose the hypocrisy of the Scribes and Pharisees and present teachings higher than theirs. Also, the words of the Lord had the spirit, while their talk had literalism and therefore they did not want to listen to it.

Stubbornness or arrogance stops the ear from hearing. Even if the view is strong and convincing, the ear will not hear it as long as the person is arrogant. Some of Christ's words, the scribes not only refused to listen to, but *"they took up stones again to stone him."* *(John 10:31)*. They described Him as pervert, deceiver and blasphemer.

Fear also blocks the ear from hearing.

Pilate believed that Christ was innocent and righteous *(Matt. 27:24),* but his fear stopped him from benefiting from the advice of his wife, *"Have nothing to do with this just man." (Matt. 27:19).*

Fear also stopped many Roman rulers from converting to faith; fear blocked their ears.

How nice is the Lord's saying to His pure disciples, *"But blessed are your ears for they hear." (Matt. 13:16).* It is the ear which its hearing comes out of a heart filled with faith, submission, love and meekness and holds the desire to listen, like Mary, the sister of Martha. The adverse kind rejects every advice and every word!

They have ears but they are not for hearing!

✙

✙ ✙ ✙

178. SELF ESTEEM

A person who is filled with self-esteem might reach a stage which could be dangerous to himself and hard to those who work with him.

He could adhere to his views and accept no argument also he will not forfeit them even if the contra opinion is convincing! He will not accept the idea of another opinion and will consider it as a big insult that his pride would reject!

It has to be only his opinion and his opinion has its impeccability which is faultless!

That is how he reaches, in his thoughts, a stage of obstinacy and stubbornness.

In such a way, those with their own ideas and all those who prefer to use their own minds will turn their back to him, leaving only a group of rebellious people who will blindly follow him in whatever he says.

The self-conceited also talks to people from above.

He thinks that he has reached a level higher than others, so he only talks to either advise, give orders, suggest or reproach them for their faults no matter who they were and what their age or positions would be!

By doing that, he could commit a mistake against others.

He might do that without paying any attention and without his conscience rebuking him, as in his self-centredness, he will never realise where he went wrong.

The self-conceited could also reach a stage of worshipping himself!!

Many are the "gods" who walk on earth!

Each of them considers himself always right. If anyone disagreed with him, the one who is wrong must be the other person.

What are the reasons for self-conceit? May be some gift granted by God but one misused and hurt himself.

Or it could be success on a specific occasion so his heart was inflated by this success and did not glorify God.

There could also be old pride in his heart and being conceited is one of its symptoms, or in his up-bringing, he was pampered in certain ways.

Whatever the reason is, humility is the only remedy for self-conceit. The fear of losing everyone also urges him to change.

✛

179.   YOU OR THE OTHERS?

God gave you your soul to be responsible for it before Him, like a steward who was entrusted with a stewardship. Are you busy with it or with others?

There is no objection if it is within the responsibility of your service, if you have a service. That also has to be done in a circle of love like that of God,*"... who desires all men to be saved and to come to the knowledge of the truth." (1 Tim. 2:4).*

There is another condition, that you do not neglect yourself, forget your eternity and put your concern for others before your concern for the purity of your heart, deepening your relationship with God and His love.

You have also to beware of the devil of grandeur that might insinuate to you the desire of managing others as if you were appointed as their guardian!

We here remember what St. John Saba says, "If you were fought with that, consider your feelings, senses and thoughts and say that is what God has entrusted me with, to manage my household well."

God gave you a power of anger to direct it to your own faults so you correct yourself and revolt against your falls. By doing this, you carry out the Lord's commandment in the psalm, *"Be angry and do not sin." (Ps. 4:4).*

As for directing your anger towards others, you will sin. And the Lord says, *"Remove the plank that is in your own eye first, then you will see clearly to remove the speck that is in your brother's eye." (Luke 6:42).*

Direct the ability to judge to yourself and not to others. If you find in yourself the tendency to criticise and look at black spots, say to yourself no objection. I have many black spots in myself that you can criticise. You would not have the time then to criticise other's faults.

I preach first in Jerusalem before I preach in Samaria and in the farther parts of the world. Look after yourself before you go very far, to others everywhere.

Be assured that by concerning yourself with your purity, spirituality and eternity, you will be then setting a good example for others and a good model. And when you are concerned with others, let it be in a spiritual manner that has no blemish in it.

180. REGRET

Many take actions that they later on regret, either due to its bad results or because their conscience troubles them and turns against them. It could also be that they fail to put matters back to the way they were before taking these wrong actions.

The regret increases more as the person realises the horror of his sin and the greatness of his guilt, just like Judas, and as Cain said, *"My punishment is greater than I can bear." (Gen. 4:13).*

The regret also increases when one realises that it is of no use. For example, a word is said and nobody can get it back, or take it out of the ears of those who heard it, no matter how the person apologises.

Wrong deeds that one regrets could be the result of rashness, hastiness and lack of consideration. It could also be due to lack of consultation before taking such action. The terrible and wrong deed could also be the outcome of anger, inner revolution, loss of self-control, ignoring the results or not giving them a thought completely.

As one regrets what he does hastily and without consultation, he may also regret giving in to his desires and passions, without putting God before him and without considering his dignity as an image of God.

One may also regret not taking the future into account when he acted carelessly in a light, and lazy manner.

Nevertheless, regret has its benefit, as it leads one to repentance, correcting his life-style. It also has another benefit, as it leads one to a life of humility and contrition. That is what happened with the prophet David, who every night, drenched his couch with his tears. It also happened to St. Paul, the Apostle, who says, *"... I am not worthy to be called an apostle, because I persecuted the Church of God."* (1 Cor. 15:9).

Regret could be of benefit here, but in eternity it turns into torment. There wouldn't be repentance, as the time of repentance would be over, "... *and the door was shut* ..." as in the parable of the foolish virgins who heard the Lord saying, *"I do not know you."* (Matt. 25:10). The regret here turned into *".. weeping and gnashing of teeth."* (Matt. 25:30).

Struggle then while you are on earth before it is too late when regret wouldn't be of benefit. That is the share of those who do not labour now, as the poet says:

If you did not sow and watched a reaper -

You shall regret for wasting the time of sowing.

181. THE CRITICAL EYE

A critical eye does not see except defects only. It does not see all the other white spots. Therefore, its judgment is not accurate or fair. It also does not give a correct picture.

A critical eye could criticise everyone without exception and nobody would be safe from it. No matter how a person may be righteous or of a sound opinion, such an eye will find something worth criticism. As the saying goes: he who searches for a defect will find it.

The critical eye lacks love and lacks humility.

A loving person does not criticise. It says in the Bible, *"love does not behave rudely, thinks no evil". (1 Cor. 13:5).*

A loving person conceals others' mistakes and does not defame them. He finds excuses for the defects and if he fails, he reproaches quietly, in an atmosphere of a useful advice.

As the loving person does not criticise much, so is the humble one. He looks to his personal faults and not to those of others.

The Lord gave us an advice, that one should look at the plank in his own eye and not at the speck in his brother's eye.

The one who has love and humility, if needs to criticise, it has to be a very special case concerning a very serious matter.

Criticism is not a permanent and constant attitude in his life and does not become part of his behaviour when dealing with others.

The critical eye criticises without gentleness and does not see anything beautiful except itself.

It sees the thorns that surround the rose and criticises that. But during the criticism, ignores the lovely fragrance of the rose.

Therefore, the critical eye is not favoured by people. Everyone is cautious of it. Everyone says, "it might befall me too!"

Very often the critical eye acts without examination or investigation. Maybe it sees a defect where there is none!

As for the just person who does not judge before examining and the kind person who does not criticise everything, knowing that perfection is only for God. Such a person would be favoured by all.

182.   YOUR RELATIONSHIP WITH THE GOOD

Your relationship with the good concentrates on three main points:

> 1 - To know what is good
> 2 - To long for it and love it
> 3 - To transform it into life

1   The knowledge of good is necessary because many sin due to ignorance, or because they stop sometimes at crossroads, not knowing which is the right one. To know what is good needs wisdom and discrimination or it needs guidance and heed.

2   The knowledge of good alone is not enough if you are not willing to follow the good path. Many are controlled by their desires although they know they are sinful ones and it will harm them. But the willingness to leave it behind does not exist inside them.

The most dangerous thing in sin is that man loves it, becomes attached to it and not willing to leave it. He knows that repentance is good but does not want it.

To make one aware that this matter is a sin, needs mental conviction. The rest is to affect his feelings, inclinations and desires, to long with his heart to what he has been convinced with in his mind.

3 Here, we move to the practical step of execution: either to start immediately if the heart was highly burning for repentance or start with spiritual practices and progress gradually.

The prodigal son was not satisfied with his conviction that he is on the wrong path and should change it. He started to carry out what he was convinced with. Then, he left and went to his father.

Those who are carried by grace might not need spiritual practices.

But the majority of people are stopped by obstacles from natural dispositions and traditions, as well as obstructions by external effects. They need an inward struggle within themselves and a struggle against the wars that come from the outside.

If one trained himself practically to be on the good path and followed it, he then has to stabilise himself and not to turn to his old behaviour. The love of good will then become part of his nature. That needs time and work of grace.

183. THEY WERE A BLESSING

There are people who lived on earth and were a blessing.

For example, our father Abraham, the father of fathers, about whom it was said, *"I will make you a great nation; I will bless you. And make your name great; and you shall be a blessing." (Gen. 12:2).*

And before our father Abraham there was our father Noah, for whose sake God retained life on earth when it was destroyed by the flood (Genesis 6). All living creatures on earth perished and humanity almost faced extinction, had it not been for Noah, who became father of humanity after Adam.

We also read in the Holy Bible about persons who were a blessing wherever they went. One of them is Joseph, the Righteous, who became a blessing in the house of Potiphar. As it says in the Bible, *"And his master saw that the Lord was with him and that the Lord made all he did to prosper in his hand. Then he made him overseer of his house and all that he had he put in his hand." (Gen. 39:3-4).*

That is how Joseph was a blessing in the land of Egypt and for his sake God saved Egypt and the surrounding countries from the famine.

The same thing happened with Elijah who was a blessing in the house of the widow.

Because of him, God blessed her oil and her flour and so, *"The bin of flour was not used up nor did the jar of oil run dry." (1 Kin. 17:16).*

The prophet Elijah was also a blessing in the house of the Shunammite. The woman felt it and knew that because of his prayers God granted her a child and through the prophet's prayers God raised her son from death.

The visit of the Virgin Mary carrying Jesus was a blessing to Egypt.

Because of this visit many of the idols in Egypt were broken and the faith entered some hearts. Later on, Churches were established in all the places they visited. The blessings of the Virgin Mary remain until today and the blessings of Jesus himself are still in our country.

We also remember the blessings of the martyrs in our country and the blessings of those who lived in solitude and the spirit borne. They blessed many places by their prayers and their holy life. These places where they lived in seclusion became visiting spots for people to receive their blessings.

That reminds us with the blessing the "ten" that God mentioned during the destruction of Sodom, *"I will not destroy it for the sake of ten." (Gen. 18:32).*

We also remember how the tithe blesses our money, if we pay it and also the blessings of the day of the Lord, if we keep it holy.

184. THREE ADVICES IN TRIBULATIONS

If you are encircled by tribulation or an affliction do not be troubled and do not let sadness or weariness control you. How easy it is to pass through an affliction with a peaceful heart and quietness if you remember the following three phrases, in depth and in faith:

God exists - All is good - Wait on the Lord.

Feeling that God exists gives you comfort as you are not on your own. There is the One who supports you, God who told us that even, *".. the very hairs of your head are all numbered."* *(Matt. 10:30).* God who loves you and defends you would not deliver you to the hands of your enemy. The Bible says, *"The Lord will fight for you and you shall hold your peace." (Exo. 14:14).*

Whatever tribulations surround you, do not worry and tell yourself, "God exists". If my enemy is strong, God is stronger and if the matter is complicated, God is capable of solving any problem. *"The things which are impossible with men are possible with God." (Luke 18:27).*

Put God between you and the trouble, it will disappear and the loving God will remain. Do not put the trouble between you and God as God's help may disappear and the trouble remains facing you, then you shall complain and grumble.

It is also a comfort to say to yourself during tribulations, "all is for good".

Joseph, the Righteous, was sold as a slave by his brothers and the wife of Potiphar accused him unjustly and he was thrown in prison. In spite of that, all was for good. They meant him evil and God meant good, so He changed the evil into good. Here, the saying of the Apostle encourages us, *"And we know that all things work together for good to those who love God." (Rom. 8:28).*

Many are the tribulations that ended good. Live them in hope and faith in the good that is about to come and not in the distress that is already here.

Pray that God may be with you and strengthen you. And if the answer was delayed, do not be annoyed and lose your peace. You'll find comfort in the Psalm that says, *"Wait on the Lord, be of good courage and he shall strengthen your heart; wait, I say, on the Lord!" (Ps. 27:14).*

It might seem that good is late but it will surely come, even in the last hour of the night, so wait with a strong heart.
Enduring tribulations is a great virtue. The one that is bigger is rejoicing during the tribulation.

185. FORMALITY OF WORSHIP

God, does not want your worship but your heart. Let worshipping be just an expression of what this heart feels.
Therefore, God blamed His people by saying, *"These people draw near to me with their mouth and honour me with their lips, but their heart is far from me." (Matt. 5:8)*.

This worship on the outside is rejected by God because He always confides to us saying, *"My son, give me your heart."* *(Prov. 23:26)*.

The people of Israel used to increase their sacrifices and burnt offerings, completing the rituals of the outside worship as fastings, feasts and celebrations, raising incense, offering prayers while their heart far from God, leading both evil and worship side by side.

Therefore, God rebuked them, saying, *"To what purpose is the multitude of your sacrifices to me? I have had enough of burnt offerings of rams and the fat of fed cattle. Bring no more futile sacrifices. Incense is an abomination to me. Your new moons and your appointed feasts My soul hates; they are a trouble to me, I am weary of bearing them. When you spread out your hands, I will hide my eyes from you; even though you make many prayers, I will not hear. Your hands are full of blood."* *(Is. 1:11-15)*.

He also said to them through Jeremiah, *"Your burnt offerings are not acceptable, nor your sacrifices sweet to me." (Jer. 6:20).* The prophet knew the reason for that, therefore he said to God, *"You are near in their mouth, but far from their mind." (Jer. 12:2).* Thus God refused their worship and, in His anger, said, *"When they fast, I will not hear their cry; and when they offer burnt offering and grain offering, I will not accept them. But I will consume them by the sword, by the famine and by the pestilence." (Jer. 14:12).*

And you, my beloved Beware of being like the tombs that are whitewashed on the outside concerning yourself with worship and rituals, sacrifices and incense, leaving aside the weight of the Law: Justice and Mercy *(Matt. 23:23).*

Do not measure your prayer by its length but by its depth and purity. The prayer of the Pharisee was longer than that of the tax collector but God did not accept him as his heart was not pure. Do not concentrate on the outside incense but purify your heart and your prayers will be set before God as incense.

186.   TROUBLESOME MESSAGES

"How beautiful are the feet of those who bring glad tidings of good things?" (Rom. 10:15).

How beautiful it is when God sends some of His saints, bringing glad tidings to people, as He sent the two Marys to announce the good news to the disciples about the Lord's holy Resurrection.

But there are other messages that are troubling, God sometimes instructs His saints to deliver them to people.   For example, when He sent the prophet Elijah to Ahab the King, saying to him, *"... in the place where dogs licked the blood of Naboth, the dogs shall lick your blood ... because you have sold yourself to do evil ..." (1 Kin. 21:19-20).*   The same with the prophet Isaiah who was sent to Ezekial the King saying, *"Set your house in order, for you shall die and not live." (Is. 38:1).*

There are messages of reproof and rebuke that God sends to people through His prophets.   It might trouble them and hurt them.   They might even hate the prophets and harm them for that reason.   But the men of God are obliged to deliver God's word and witness for it, no matter how painful it is.

The prophet Jeremiah is such an example.   He lived in Egypt during a period of complete corruption.   He had to rebuke everyone: *"The rulers, the priests and those who handle the* law." *(Jer. 2:8)*. They turned against him and roused the people saying, *"This man deserves to die." (Jer. 26:11)*.

Many are the prophets who were stoned and killed for a just word that people found troubling for them. The Lord rebuked Jerusalem saying, *"O Jerusalem, Jerusalem the one who kills the prophets and stones those who are sent to her." (Matt. 23:37)*.

Therefore, Jeremiah the prophet cried saying, *"Woe is me, my mother, that you have borne me, a man of strife and a man of contention to the whole earth!" (Jer. 15:10)*. Everybody turned against him because he carried to them God's word of rebuke and warning.

The false prophets that Jeremiah had to fight used to flatter the people by saying, *"Peace, peace!: when there is no peace." (Jer. 8:11)*.

As for the prophet of God, he used to deliver the divine message which was troubling but useful. So were the prophets of Baal who flattered Ahab, the evil and encouraged him in his sinful way, the exact opposite of Micaiah, the man of God. Therefore, Ahab said about him to Jehoshaphat when advised to ask God, *"There is still one man, Micaiah the son of Imlah, by whom we may inquire of the Lord; but I hate him, because he does not prophesy good concerning me, but evil." (1 Kin. 22:8)*. Ahab listened to the flatterers and not Micaiah's honest opinion and perished. It would have been better for him to listen to Micah's troubling, but useful message!!

187.   WRONG RULES

What we experience during the feasts of the martyrs and the Feasts of the Cross, with all the beautiful meaning that they indicate about strength, is a reminder of other wrong rulings:

Who was stronger: the Crucified Jesus or the Jews who crucified Him?!

The Lord Jesus experienced various types of humiliation, was flogged, hanged on a piece of timber but He was strong in His crucifixion, capable of defeating sin and the devil and opening the gates of paradise. He was stronger than those who crucified Him, who were defeated by the sins of injustice, the cruelty, envy and false witnessing!

Who was stronger: Cain, the murderer or Abel, the murdered?

Cain managed to throw Abel on the ground and murder him. Nevertheless, Cain was not strong. The sins of envy, hatred and cruelty overcame (defeated) him. As for Abel, the murdered, he was much higher than that.

Often a conqueror thinks he is victorious and shows off in vanity and self-admiration while in reality he is defeated.
He is defeated by himself who could not overcome its desires and defeated by other sins and wrong rules that enabled him to

image victory where there is only defeat! The same with the one who, when he strikes you on the right cheek, you offer him the other also.

Do you think he has defeated you?! No. His anger, fury and lack of respect for others defeated him. The same with the one who insults and humiliates you. Poor fellow, he thinks he is stronger than you. His heart and his tongue defeated him.

Everyone in this world could get angry, abuse and attack others. But the strong one is that who controls his temper, his tongue, his senses and endures.

The one who endures is the stronger. Therefore, the Apostle says, *"We then who are strong ought to bear with the scruples of the weak." (Rom. 15:1).*

Does Herod think that he was stronger than John the Baptist because he offered John's head on a plate?!

Definitely not. The murdered was stronger. Herod remained in fear of John even after he was beheaded. And when Jesus appeared, Herod thought it was John risen from the dead.

How amazing are peoples' rulings! They think it is strength when it is nothing but weakness! They think it is victory when it is nothing but defeat. They are wrong rules.

My brother, triumph over yourself. The one who defeats himself is better than the one who defeats a city.

188.   THE ELEMENT OF MEMORISING

You can use part of your leisure time in memorising.

By that we mean memorising psalms, prayers, verses or extracts from the Holy Bible, tunes and hymns or chants from the book of chants "Absalmodia" and others.

There is a phrase that I repeatedly said to many: "Keep the psalms (in your memory), the psalms will keep you. Keep the Bible, the Bible will keep you."

The practice of memorising is not only to occupy leisure time where one spends spiritual time, contemplating on the meaning and depth of what he memorises, but also for many other benefits.

By memorising, one would be able to complete his prayers at any time and in any position and any place; amongst people, without the need of a book to open exposing his prayers before others! By memorising, one would be able to pray while walking in the street or riding means of transport or while with people talking about matters that do not concern him. He would sit quietly as if listening to them while he is praying in his heart secretly without anyone noticing it.

By memorising one would be able to pray in darkness and would be able to keep himself busy when on a trip or a long walk.

What he learns while memorising could be used while serving or giving a sermon and to resist thoughts and combats. It also keeps the mind pure, occupied with God.

As a suggested programme for memorising, one could start with parts that are common in Agbia [The Book of the Seven Prayers] such as the prayer of Thanksgiving, Psalm 50, the Trisagion, Holy, Holy, Holy, Have mercy on us, O Lord, then some psalms according to one's choice, parts of the hours' prayers, their Gospel and Absolution.

As for the young ones: they could memorise many short verses according to the Alphabetical order, some hymns, Church tunes as they love music and chants. Then they could memorise some prayers from Agbia or psalms to match with their level.
Competitions could be held by Sunday School and youth groups, giving gifts to outstanding competitors and certificates of recognition.

189. BEAKING THE MIRRORS

As the body looks attentively to its image in the mirror, to make sure it is all right, so does the soul. It has many mirrors where it could consider its image and knows in what stage it is.

There is a mirror called "judging oneself". If one searched within himself and was strict in judging it, then he will know its reality and reform it.

Another mirror is, "Words of God". One sees himself in the light of God's commandments, knows the real scale with which to weigh his deeds.

There is another mirror, that is "tribulations", because through tribulations we are tested.

The fourth mirror is "people's criticism". Many a time one favours himself, justifying its deeds. As for people, they do not favour. They might speak frankly, so we know our true self from them. Even if we get angry with them, we would realise another side of ourselves, that is anger. In that way, the mirror would have done its job.

These are the mirrors in which one sees his real self. But some people, if the mirror uncovers a defect in them that needs mending, instead of correcting what is wrong, they break the mirror!

These people, if self-judgment uncovered a defect, they refuse to sit with themselves. And if they do, they break the mirror by excuses, self-justification and trying to put the blame on others!

If the words of God showed a defect in them, they break this mirror too by applying God's words to others not to themselves or they refuse reading these words. If trials uncovered their reality, they break the mirror by murmuring!

They also break the fourth mirror, rejecting a word of criticism from anyone, not even an advice or a word of guidance. Whoever points out a defect that could be mended, they consider him an enemy, they fight him and try to destroy him until he is silent, then they shall be satisfied.

Those who break mirrors, their faults remain as they were without being corrected.

It is like a person suffering from fever. He puts the thermometer in his mouth. If it shows a high temperature, instead of treating himself, breaks the thermometer and remains ill! The poor, honest thermometer is just like the other broken mirrors!!!

190. USING AUTHORITY

During the Lord's temptation on the mountain, the devil said to Him, *"If you are the Son of God, command that these stones become bread." (Matt. 4:3).* The Lord Jesus Christ could have transformed the stones into bread. He is capable of raising children for Abraham from stones and He is the One who said to the Jews when He entered Jerusalem in answer to their protest against the children praise, *".. if these should keep silent, the stones would immediately cry out." (Luke 19:40).*

The Lord Jesus Christ had already put before himself an important principle, that is not to use His divinity for the comfort of His body. He could have used His divine power to stop Himself from experiencing hunger, thirst, getting tired or feeling pain. If He did that, His incarnation would have been formal!! Therefore, the Lord refused to use His Divinity for His bodily comfort.

He used His Divinity for the comfort of people as in the miracle of feeding the multitude from five loaves.

The Lord's decision also indicates another determination, that is not to use authority generally, except when necessary. The Jews attacked Him in various ways: insulted Him, humiliated Him and called Him gluttonous and a wine-bibber, that by Beelzebub He casts demons, that He is a Samaritan, possessed by a demon, that He profanes the Sabbath, breaks the Law, blasphemer and deceptive. He used to hear and remain silent. He never used His authority to punish them.

On the contrary, when His two disciples insisted on punishment, He refused and considered it a repetition of the temptation on the mountain or another effort by the devil to make Him use His authority for Himself. It happened when one of the Samaritan cities refused to accept him. His two disciples said to Him, *"Lord, do you want us to command fire to come down from heaven and consume them?" (Luke 9:54).* The Lord replied in reproach, *"You do not know what manner of spirit you are of." (Luke 9:55).*

The Lord preferred to always avoid using His authority. Many are those who blaspheme against Him now in our days and many are those who deny His existence. Many are also those who defy His orders, accuse and mock. God leaves all these, without punishing and without destroying!!

All those who provoke for a fire to come down from heaven and consume these and those, the Lord will answer by the same phrase, "You do not know what manner of spirit you are of."

191. THOSE WORKING WITH THE LORD

It is enough for one to be certain that he works with God then after that he should not have any worry. The Lord that he works with will work out everything.

We do not defend ourselves, as the Bible says, *"The Lord will fight for you and you shall hold your peace" (Exo. 14:14), "War is for God"* and *"The Lord executes justice for the oppressed"* and He *"establishes justice on earth".*

We do not support ourselves. God is the One who cares for everyone. He is the One who lets the water flow from the rock and *"out of the eater came something to eat and out of the strong came something sweet." (Judg. 14:14).* He satisfies the needs of all who live from His grace and *".. gives to the beast its food and to the young ravens that cry." (Ps. 147:9).*

We do not protect ourselves, because, *"Unless the Lord builds the house, they labour in vain who build it. Unless the Lord guards the city, the watchman stays awake in vain." (Ps. 127:1).*

God is everything we have. He is our whole life. He organises everything. We are just tools in His hands. We do His work, but we do not work from ourselves. He works in us, He works through us and with us.

The Lord opens and nobody shuts, He shuts and nobody opens. He provides for the universe, not the human. He is wise in his provision. We see the work of the Lord and rejoice. We do not question what He does, but be glad because He works.

Happy is the one who works with the Lord and could see how God looks after everything.

God is the Almighty who controls all. He created the universe but did not leave it. He still provides for it by Himself in wisdom and justice. He might leave people for their free will, to do what they like. But, *"... a book of remembrance is written before Him." (Mal. 3:16).* Then He interferes to establish justice on earth.

How wonderful you are, God. Who is like You?! We have felt Your hand in everything we do, so we abandoned our life for You in confidence. We fear nothing and we fear nobody, because You are with us. You are the hope of the hopeless and the help of the helpless.

192. THE ABANDONMENT OF GRACE

Success or failure in one's spiritual life depends on the work of grace and the extent of one's acceptance or refusal of it.

Grace always helps man, assists him in leading a spiritual path, warns and lifts him up if he falls.

The divine grace does not force man to do good.

His free will is still in power, sharing in the work with grace or not; resisting the work of grace until he falls or continues in his fall.

Therefore, one sometimes abandons sharing in the work of grace. Sometimes grace abandons him. But it is a kind of partial abandonment. Complete abandonment would definitely lead to one's destruction.

What are the reasons for this abandonment? What is the wisdom behind it?

The reason for the abandonment could be negligence on the side of the faithful and continual rejection of the work of grace. Therefore, grace abandons him until he feels the need for it.

This abandonment leads to greater depth in one's prayers and fastings, repentance and attachment to God.

Pride could be the reason for this abandonment, or it could be one's superiority over those who have fallen. Grace would then leave him for a little while so he would fall, realise his weakness and stop his arrogance. He would also feel the heaviness of war against those who fall and have sympathy on them instead of judging them with secrecy or in the open. Grace might forsake one for a while to experience spiritual combats and realise its depth and the faithfuls need for the divine support, as one would never win by relying on a human hand without grace.

Grace might also forsake a person to get him accustomed to cautiousness and scrutiny, patience and victory of the Lord.

During all that, the Lord says to the human soul, *"For a mere moment I have forsaken you, but with great mercies I will gather you." (Is. 54:7).*

193. DEFINITIONS

Many ideological disagreements could be solved if we reach a correct definition for some of the words that are the subject of disagreement.

1. For example, what is the correct definition of the word "freedom"?

   Does it mean one does whatever he likes without control?

   Or does it mean one should act freely but should not violate the freedom of others or break the general order?

   If we realise that the last definition is acceptable, then we get into another definition, that is: the conditions mentioned before, would they be considered limits of the freedom or restraints? If we consider it restraints, then there would not be disagreement about the meaning of freedom.

2. Another matter needs scrutiny in understanding, that is:

   What is the correct definition of obedience? Is it blind obedience?

   Some confession fathers enforce obedience that abolishes the personality of the confessor? They do not give him a chance to discuss what is said to him. They might consider such a discussion as a kind of insolence! Then he will do what is not accepted by his thought or by his conscience!

We do not accept the obedience that the conscience turns against, because: "We ought to obey God rather than men." (Acts 5:29).

Obedience then is necessary, but within God's commandments.

The discussion between the follower and the guide should not be considered as insolence.

3. Disagreements arise in the subject of faith and deeds, due to the definition:

   If we understand the meaning of "deeds", the disagreement will dissolve. Are they the deeds before the faith or the deeds of the Law, or the human hand or these deeds are in communion with the Holy Spirit after faith? Also, what is faith? Is it the one who works with love?

4. "Man", the name itself, needs to be defined. And many matters depend on this definition.

   If we realise that man is a living creature with an immortal soul and that his life extends after his death, then one should prepare himself for eternal life and respect his humanity. Therefore, he has to be defined as the image of God. Many other matters need to be defined, such as: what is sin? What is pleasure? What is love?

194. LIMITS

On the spiritual path, a traffic officer stands with two flags in his hand, one green and the other red, to indicate who should pass and who should not, putting limits between what is lawful and what is unlawful.

There are many questions in one's mind concerning this matter.

1 For example, what are the spiritual limits between silence and talk? When should one remain silent and when should he talk? When would silence be considered a virtue and when would one be judged for it?

2 Joking, for example: When to beware of it? When is it unlawful? What are the limits that separate between innocent joking and that which is not innocent?

3 The same when separating between resting and idleness, between firmness and cruelty, between love and lust, between literality and scrutiny, between humility and being mean-spirited???

4 Other questions about the limits: When is it lawful for one to complain and when is it not? When is it lawful for one spiritually to ask for his rights and when does he give it up and not ask for it?

When do we rebuke sinners? When does this rebuke become harmful for them?

Would that traffic officer raise one of the flags and give the direction? Where are the limits between good and evil in the midst of blurred vision?

5 The one who committed suicide, was he aware of what he was doing? Should the Church pray for the one who killed a soul? Or was he completely unconscious and is clear of the responsibility?

6 The same with this question: Does a child know what he is doing? Should we question him or treat him as one who knows? Or should we let it simply pass as if he has done nothing?

Where is good? Where is justice? Where is the duty of the educator?

7 Sometimes, the confessor comes to his spiritual guide and says: I do not know what to do, a the guide may stand in the same bewilderment!

How could he guide him? The good is not clearly showing! He would then say, "Let us pray, my son, until God shows us."

What a difficult job is that of the judge, the guide and the educator! How difficult it is too, the job of the traffic officer? When should he let the traffic go without an accident, making sure that the road will be leading?

195. THE ATTRACTION OF NUMBER

Many get attracted to number, any number!

They think that success in life depends on the number.

Some priests are delighted because of the number of those who confess, or the number of those who come to Church and not with the number of repentants among them. Maybe those who repent are very few!

Many Sunday School servants are happy with the number of their students. Many preachers also think the measure of their success is the number of those who attend their meetings while many of these listeners may have never carried out any of what they heard in their personal spiritual life.

The number is not a measure of success. The real measure is the depth and spirituality and whatever concerns salvation of the soul.

Then what is important is not the number of prostrates (Metania) that you do everyday but the spiritual manner in which they are done. Is it with a contrite heart, accompanied by ardent prayers? Or isn't like that?

The number of Chapters you read in the Bible is not important, but it is the understanding, contemplation and application.

It is not the amount but the spirituality of the fasting.
The outside appearance is no judge in spiritual matters. The number is no doubt an outside appearance. But the fair judgment is the heart and the spirit and how they are connected to God.

The temptation of the number could be a war from the self!

The self that thinks it might get bigger because of the number!

The Lord Jesus Christ concentrated on a few disciples, just twelve, then another seventy. He could have had thousands. The twelve were more powerful than thousands. They were a lesson to us for concentration.

When would the time come where we care for the perfected few more that the many without perfection.

If the two matters are combined, then it is good and a blessing.

196. OCCASIONS TO SEIZE

There are important occasions that pass by and one should stop there, not letting it depart easily without taking a decision that would raise his spirituality and his relationship with God. We mention here:

The beginning of the new year or a new year in his life.

The beginning of the Holy Fast.

A specific incident that affected him and shook his inside.

An illness that left him bedridden, thinking about his destiny.

A serious problem that faced him, so he turned to the Divine help.

A sermon that he heard or read and it strongly attracted him to God.

All these occasions usually carry the voice of God, who calls with the Apostle saying, *"If you will hear his voice, do not harden your hearts." (Heb. 3:8).*

These occasions could also carry one of the visits of grace, seeking one's soul should to wake up and heed.

If one received it carelessly or with momentary effect that ends with the end of the occasion, then he will definitely lose spiritual feelings that he might never find again. He will then say in regret, missing God's voice, *"But my beloved had turned away and was gone. I sought him, but I could not find him." (Song 5:6)*.

Truly, how many occasions passed by without us seizing them?! How many spiritual revivals God called us to, without us seizing them?!

The grace is present, working in us and we do not respond to it! It is really a tragedy, that love between us and god is a one sided love, on God's side only!

"Therefore, you are inexcusable, O man!" (Rom. 2:1). Do not say that God has left you and did not send a helping hand to your life with Him. God has talked in your heart repeatedly and you did not hear or respond. Is He going to force you to love Him?!

In your relationship with God, it should be a spontaneous love that does not need such occasions!

At least, if this love went to sleep, let us hear on such occasions a voice that wakes it up and if it grew lukewarm, to find what inflames it.

"He who has ears to hear, let him hear!" (Matt. 11:15).

197.   YOUR NATURE

Do not say when you sin: What can I do, it is my evil nature!

Your nature is not evil. Evil is an intruder.

God created man pure and simple to the extent that Adam and Eve were naked in Paradise without being aware of it, *"and they were both naked". (Gen. 2:25).*

Then Adam and Eve fell through the temptation of the serpent and not because of their evil nature. And man knew evil. And evil remained an intruder as it was never part of his original nature.

Jesus then sanctified our nature when he became unified with it in the Virgin's womb. And this nature was renewed in the baptistery with the worthiness of the holy blood.

We became members in the body of Christ, which is the Church and became a dwelling for the Holy Spirit in the sacrament of the holy anointment. We received the gifts of the new Testament that were not for us before. Evil remained an intruder.

Truly, how beautiful is the priest's saying in the Liturgy of St. Gregory, "My nature was blessed in You." And so it became a blessed nature.

Truly, it is still a nature that could drift, due to the free will. But this inclination is not forced on it and falling is not part of its characteristics. The will could be directed to the good.

With this human nature, our fathers the saints were able to reach high levels in loving God, with our same nature.

One could here read lives of the monks and recluses, the spirit-borne, the martyrs, the confessors and heroes of faith and stories about the righteous in all ages, those who lived in celibacy or those who married.

Even those who drifted and fell, the same nature helped them to repent and grew to high levels of a life of holiness.

These repentant's cast away evil that was an intruder in their nature and returned to the purity that God created in them since the beginning and even turned to the holiness that God wished for them.

Sin might spoil your nature and falling repeatedly might make sin part of your characteristics but not your nature. This remains as an intruder on the image that God created for you and turned you back to it.

Return to this holy image, it is your original nature.

198. REPEATED FALLING

Due to man's weakness, he might fall, as he is not infallible. But he has to repent and learn a lesson from his fall, so he wouldn't fall again, as said by one of the saints, "I don't recall the devils making me fall in the same sin twice."

This is real repentance, as one does not go back to the sin that he has repented. All the stories of the repentant saints refer to this meaning: that repentance was a line separating between two lives and they never turned back to their old sinful life.

It is not true repentance when one, every time he repents, keeps on falling repeatedly, as if he has not repented!

Repeated falling has its danger and its indication.

It shows the lack of seriousness in one's life with God. It may also indicate carelessness and lack of interest in the spiritual principles.

It is also an evidence that the heart has not been purified yet and it still has the love of sin, with weakness and attraction to it.

Repeated falling proves the lack of understanding confessing one's sin, as if it is just a way to get out of the punishment for this sin without getting rid of the sin itself.

Repeated falling makes one lose his dignity before the devils. It gives them authority over him as they discover his incapability to resist sin, or his unwillingness to leave it!

Repeated falling could change the sin into a habit, or characteristic and could make its roots in the heart and the mind.

By repeating the sin, it remains in the subconscious and becomes a source of dreams, thoughts, doubts and desires. It could also become dangerous for the person, if it turns into unconscious deeds or slavery to sin!!

Every time one falls, his will gets weaker.

His ability to live a righteous life becomes less. Thus he becomes less affected by the spiritual means, or refuses to accept them!

In spite of all that, the grace of God is always ready to raise him, if he wishes. But the way to repentance becomes harder.

199.   HESITATION

Hesitation is a psychological disease or a weakness in the personality.

St. James, the Apostle, says, *"He is a double-minded man, unstable in all his ways." (James 1:8).*

The one who hesitates might say I am thinking and studying.
But there is a big difference between thinking in depth and being hesitant.

There is a difference between the one who studies in depth and the one who, after deciding on one thing, changes his mind to another then goes back to the first one and leaves it later on, without settling on any.

Maybe hesitation is due to fear and fear has its reasons. It could be the fear of failure or acting wrongly that is causing hesitation.   It could be fear because of weakness and incapability, or the fear of results and responsibility. It could also be the fear of choosing badly and more than one solution is being offered.

As one in cross-roads, afraid of choosing a road that gets him lost!

Hesitation could also be due to lack of self-confidence.

Maybe the hesitant is one who is not used to depend on himself and has no self-confidence.

Therefore, he does not trust his thinking, his decision or his good choice. He also does not trust his capability. He has no experience to trust in himself. Maybe he lacks the knowledge to trust in himself. He is the image of a man.

The reason for hesitation could also be for lack in courage and valour.

He is unable to make a decision. Every time he progresses, his courage fails him. Usually, his will would be weak. Whenever he decides on a matter, he finds that everything looks the same and fails to choose one. He is not sure of the results and maybe of the means also.

Hesitation causes confusion, maybe due to lack of understanding.

He may have two matters, both are good. But which one is better? Or both are bad, but which one is less bad? Or maybe he is faced with a matter that he does not know if it is good or bad? The vision is blurred.

The reason for hesitation could also be due to many advisers and consultants.

He who has one adviser finds it easy to take one path. As for the one who asks many, there is a chance each of them leads him to a way different from the other, or gives him advice that contradicts that of another. Therefore, he stands hesitantly between contradicting advice, not knowing which is better.

Contradictory readings could also be the cause of his confused thinking.

200.   THE OTHER PARTY

If you want to be just in your judgments on people, you should always listen to the other party and not to take facts from one side only.

Everyone has the right to explain his situation. He has also the right to defend himself against all accusations. We should not pass a judgment on anyone by just listening to what has been said about him.

Maybe the one who talked against him did not see for himself or hear from a trusted source. Or maybe he misunderstood the matter. He could have also added to what he heard, his personal comment and speculations. These could all be wrong and there are circumstances that he does not know.

If a woman says that her husband treats her badly, ask her: Why? What have you done to deserve such treatment? Then ask the other side: What happened? Why? And so you form a complete picture about the matter and would have listened to both parties.

Imagine God Himself, who knows everything, asking Eve, Adam and the serpent before passing His judgment. He also asked Cain.

He gave the other party the chance to talk for himself, explain his situation and defend himself if he wanted.

Asking the other party is not meant only to know the truth with all its sides or to know the circumstances and reasons.

Asking the other party could give him a chance to apologise or correct his situation and work out the results of his action, adding understanding to his own.

When Abigail spoke to David, she gave him a chance to change his mind and not to revenge for himself, *"..You have kept me from coming to bloodshed and from avenging myself with my own hand." (1 Sam. 25:33).* He confessed, saying, *"I have sinned against the Lord." (2 Sam. 12:13).*

In your relationship with people, try to understand the other party even if he opposes you. Understand his point of view, his mentality and his psychology. You'll then know how to deal with him.

Do not always look to the other party as an enemy. Try to study his point, understand him and reach a solution, in love.

INDEX

The following is an index to all of
the volumes in the set

WORDS OF SPIRITUAL BENEFIT

each volume contains 50 Words.

Volume I	Words	1-50
Volume II	Words	51-100
Volume III	Words	101-150
Volume IV	Words	151-200

INDEX TO VOLUME I

Index to Volume II

Index to Volume III

Index to Volume IV

www.ingramcontent.com/pod-product-compliance
Lightning Source LLC
Chambersburg PA
CBHW060940120626
46557CB00003B/1079